Advanced Comprehension at the Doctor Awesome English Academy

Praise for *Advanced Comprehension at the Doctor Awesome English Academy*

"If you're expecting a collection of interconnected short stories about a dysfunctional ESL academy to be dry stuff, that's only because you haven't read Timothy Laurence Marsh yet. These short, nearly frantic dissections of grammar, trauma, lust, addiction, and ambition successfully balance Marsh's biting wit with a deep undercurrent of sadness, resulting in narratives that are as richly lyrical as they are haunting."

~ Michael Meyerhofer, author of *What To Do If You're Buried Alive*

"What comes across in these pages is a restless, riveting intelligence, along with some superb prose. This is fine work, and Marsh is a writer to keep your eye on. An enormously impressive debut."

~ Steve Yarbrough, author of *The Realm of Last Chances* and *Safe from the Neighbors*

"These stories are funny and sad and familiar despite their exotic locale, and they illuminate the mysteries of the human condition."

~ Beth Lordan, author of *And Both Shall Row* and *But Come Ye Back*

Advanced Comprehension at the Doctor Awesome English Academy
Copyright © 2026 Timothy Laurence Marsh

Front Cover by Wave

The font used is Times New Roman
The cover font is Copperplate Gothic Bold Regular

All rights reserved. No duplication or reuse of any selection is allowed without the express written consent of the publisher.

> Gnashing Teeth Publishing
> 242 East Main Street
> Norman AR 71960
> http://GnashingTeethPublishing.com

Printed in the United States of America

ISBN 978-1-966075-22-6

Gnashing Teeth Publishing First Edition

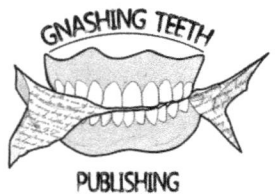

For my mother. "It's alright to get up to no good," you said. "As long as some good comes out of it."

A History of Awesomeness

Once there were three Korean businessmen who wanted what most businessmen want: to escalate their net worth, own Tour-caliber golf clubs, and tempt the appetite of the prettiest, most enviable mates. It was 2007 and Korea was manufacturing English at a pace which would've checked the ego of any industrial superpower. From Jeju to the DMZ, immersion schools and cram centers burst to life like spring cherry blossoms. Quick as cat pounce, the businessmen wrangled a group of investors, leased an office space in downtown Seoul, and founded what was sure to be the next big thing in private, for-profit English instruction.

First order of business was creating a name that would sparkle like Sirius in their cosmos of competitors. One of the businessmen liked the idea of using the word "doctor" since doctors were trusted by parents and known for fixing problems. Early iterations included the Doctor English Language Clinic and Dr. English Emergency Improvement Center. But such names felt overly corrective, if not threatening. What they needed was a splash of commercial spunk, something to capture the prodigious sensation of western pop culture. The businessmen binged on western television, gorged on western movies, and noted one exclamation repeatedly appearing in moments of pleasure and thrill. The matter was settled. From thereon their school would be known as the Doctor Awesome English Academy. Trustworthy, stylish, fun.

Next order of business was hiring a dozen support staff to devise and market a foreign language program. The staff consisted entirely of English-speaking Korean females who hadn't found husbands and could be expected to work 60-hour weeks and forsake their dinner plans for strategic development meetings. The businessmen were unequivocal: image was everything. The school bought ad space in subway tunnels, bus stops, and filled the spaces with stock posters of dandified young Anglos guiding Asian learners in the classroom, pointing exuberantly at grammar rules on whiteboards. Printed on each ad was the Doctor Awesome promise: "Preparing students for a global market where English is vital for success." Everyone agreed it was a handsome mission statement. Recruiting qualified instructors who could carry out that mission? That was another set of chopsticks.

Amongst the new hires was a freshly impregnated Mi-Hyun Choi, who'd impressed the businessmen during interviews with her ability to make a child with a western ex-pat. The businessmen had a hunch that such a person, by virtue of crossing interracial barriers in the most intimate way possible, would have unique insight into western temperament and be equipped to manage the cultural hiccups sure to arise in an international workplace.

Mi-Hyun didn't know anything special about western temperament. The only reason she'd applied to the school was to learn more about the cultural hiccups occurring in her own life. Two years into marriage and her husband still couldn't speak Korean or tell a taxi driver where to go. He drank too much, spent too much time at ex-pat bars, and now that she was pregnant he had begun to talk about leaving his ESL job in Korea and attending full moon parties in Thailand. Submitting her application, Mi-Hyun had hoped for a role free of preoccupying involvement, one that would permit her to sit behind a cloak of trifling clerical duty and observe the western teachers, especially the western men.

so she might get a sense of how better to coexist with her own western man. It didn't happen.

The businessmen were so pleased with her background they put her in charge of foreign recruitment altogether. The distinction made Mi-Hyun nauseous. She envisioned herself responsible for a rigorous seek-and-appraise process in which she had neither the experience nor communication skills to orchestrate. But the businessmen made it easy. They laid out a simple four-point measuring stick for Doctor Awesome faculty: young, white, pretty, cheap. And it was by this route Mi-Hyun discovered her husband belonged to a unique community of educators in Korea. Interviewing prospective teachers from Canada or the States she sensed the same pretexts she found in her husband. A likeable but not wholly mature manner. An emphatic but not thoroughly competent attitude. A polite but not totally committed interest in her country.

Years later, having acquired their titanium drivers and knockout wives, the three businessmen sold the school to other young businessmen seeking the same prize. One by one all the original staff found the unpaid labor of households and husbands to replace their underpaid office careers. Only Director Choi remained, moored in awesomeness.

Over the years she has watched the academy grow prevalent, not quite profitable or outstanding, but easily seen around Seoul. Despite her seniority she still handles recruitment. While she's lost precise count, figuratively speaking she takes responsibility for bringing no less than a Boeing 737's worth of western influence into her country. Few of us ever stay for long, she says. And some of us – well, some of us arouse quite a bit of regret before we leave.

Classroom Management

Erect in their seats, attentive as owls, the students wait with their lesson books open. Chapter 5: Advanced Verb Forms.

Before them stands the pride of Wayne State University, just back from a ten-minute bathroom break, three drips of piss on the knee of his pants.

It's been a rough morning for Wayne State. The shadow of last night's shitshow engulfs his face from ear to ear, thick as clown makeup. Bludgeoned by hangover, he struggles to conceal his tottering. One hand braces against the whiteboard while the other, shaky with dehydration, writes out phrasal verb combos with a dry erase marker, dragging the examples out of his brain one warped, irregular letter at a time.

Were it Tuesday or Thursday life would be cake for Wayne State. On those days his students are elementary level, easily preoccupied by language games and interactive cartoons. But today is Monday: enhanced English for pre-college learners. The students are worried about their exams, their proficiency, the expectations of their parents. They would like to excel.

Occasionally. when the grief of consciousness becomes too much, Wayne State will stop and squeeze the inner corners of his eyes with his thumb and forefinger. He is oblivious to his muttering, to his larded incoherence in general, and squints as he writes, each word as blinding and distant as the sun. The more he perseveres the worse it gets. His sentences stumble downward across the board. Words are misspelled, erased roughly with the side of his fist, misspelled again.

The students strain to make sense of the lesson, faces scrunched in concentration. Little Sun-mi Jang, who dreams of Princeton admission, is so petrified by confusion that she does not blink. At last, unwilling or unable to function any longer, Wayne State plops down at his desk. With twenty minutes left in the period he assures the class they have mastered verbs and can spend the rest of the time reviewing amongst themselves. The next moment he is doubled over, face down in his folded arms. The students, confounded by the encouraging assessment, remain quiet and staring.

About Us

With thirteen campuses conveniently situated across Seoul, the Doctor Awesome English Academy is the ideal solution to all your second-language needs. You will find our campus in the fashionable Sinchon-dong district, on the second floor of a three-story commercial building. On the ground level sits a Kentucky Fried Chicken. Above, the Mega Fun Karaoke Lounge. In between it is all Awesome.

Here at the Sinchon branch we believe in a globalized learning experience. Our friendly, enthusiastic teachers come from all corners of the English-speaking world, offering an ocean of cultural connection points. Chat about koalas with a genuine Aussie. Learn about The Beatles from a real Brit. Talk with a bona fide American about the coolest Hollywood celebs. In addition to native fluency you can be sure our faculty will be vivaciously Anglo and a pleasure to abide. Our smiles stretch forever, our accents will delight. From grade schoolers to corporate executives, students always appreciate the way our English looks.

The best part of the Doctor Awesome experience? We make learning fun! Whether you're looking to brush up on your business conversation or preparing for that big entrance exam, our passionate and professional staff is your gateway to understanding. What are you waiting for?

Start your classes today and let us make your English journey something awesome to remember.

Faculty Profile

At the Purple Haze rock bar Andy House tells his origin story.

Born in Worst Town, Missouri, to a marijuana grower and a Chickasaw housekeeper, he left home after high school and died three years later at a tequila cantina in west Texas. He'd been shooting pool with an unemployed trucker with a flaming poker hand inked on his neck. The two had been running their mouths all night, talking trash about each other's mothers and dick sizes. One taunt led to another until finally someone suggested a drinking contest to settle the discussion. Hard liquor, no chasers.

One look at that gut-busting bison of a man and Andy knew it was a bad idea. But the smack had been talked, the event set into motion, and before he could back out a table had been cleared and a bottle of tequila was between them.

From there he didn't remember much. The floor of the cantina covered in peanut shells. He remembered that. And Johnny Cash on the stereo singing about watching a man die in Reno. The two went shot for shot, one bottle then another – Andy getting so obliterated that he wet himself in the chair. But the place kept whooping and hollering, and that meaty bison kept egging him on, and so Andy kept pouring tequila into his face. Halfway through the second bottle his body started to shake and his skin went cold. The world blurred and spun. Then his head fell into his lap and he barfed so hard his nose bled. Vomited and vomited until at last he toppled out of his chair and collapsed on the floor, face down in a mess of peanut shells.

The owner had him carried outside and dumped behind the building. They slapped his face and shook his shoulders. Someone poured water on his head. Then someone noticed he wasn't breathing and called 911.

What happened after that, no wisdom can guess. For two minutes in the ambulance his consciousness vanished from existence. No pulse, no brain waves. The paramedics even noted the time of death. Then, just as they were sliding the sheet over his face, his circuitry rebooted and his brain zapped to life. They pumped his stomach at the hospital, filled his veins with hydration, and the next day he was cleared for release.

There were complications, of course. Afterward he developed problems with his vision. Sometimes he forgot he was speaking and stared into space. His left hand tingled, his left arm twitched. One day he woke up and the left side of his face had gone numb forever.

Yet from that day forward he became possessed by a new vitality. All his life he'd been told there was something beyond death. Something that burned and tormented or granted bliss and grace. But in the two minutes he'd departed existence there'd been nothing. He had not passed through time and space and arrived in a realm of spirits or seen the secrets of the universe unveiled. The lights had simply gone off. He'd read somewhere once that life was just a thin sliver of light between two immensities of darkness. Now he felt the truth of that sincerely. What else was there to do but make that sliver burn as brightly as possible?

So it happened his life became devoted to intensity. Decency, stability, success – none of that mattered anymore. For ten years he wandered the Midwest experimenting with different psychedelics, entangling with different women. He directed almost all his vitality toward drugs and women, both of which had a way of enflaming his sliver. To get by he worked at gas stations and highway sex shops because these were the places where he was apt to intersect with folk like him: rascals and storm riders, degenerates and desperados, the purposeless prowlers of earth. One night at a hostel in Sioux City he found himself smoking hash with some Canadian backpackers. The Canadians were exploring America, but their lives and jobs were in Asia.

"What's your job?" Andy asked.

"We teach," the Canadians said.

"Teach what?" asked Andy.

"English," said the Canadians.

"Like literature?"

"No. Like English."

The Canadians took out their phones and showed pictures of their lives in Asia. Photos of bars and blacklit discos that featured bottles of whisky and Barbie-dolled girls bunched around tables, their slim waists bandaged in candy-colored mini-skirts. Along with the pictures were rollicking anecdotes of personal flourishing. Way over there on the Asian side of the earth the money was good, the living cheap, the women sheltered and easy to seduce. Ah, yes. There was a future in the far east, they said. Some freshly-tapped Zen was overflowing and any bohemian soul could stake a claim and hit emotional paydirt. Andy was sold.

He enrolled in an online degree program and within three years had a diploma in Communications. Scanning the online job boards he was surprised by the number of teaching gigs which could seemingly be filled by any western degree-holder who could fog a mirror. Hundreds of schools across Asia seeking candidates with no classroom experience, no bilingual ability. Just a native tongue and a passion for education. One day a language school in Korea spotted his resume online and got in touch. The school had a silly name that didn't make sense, but it hardly mattered. It was the first gig to contact him and he took the position as soon as they offered it.

 Not long before leaving America Andy rambled back to Missouri to visit his mother. His father had long since hit the road and she lived alone with her diabetes, cable television and oxycodone. They split a joint on the porch and he broke the news about Korea as they watched the interstate across the yard and the whoosh of eighteen-wheelers. She asked what he'd be doing and he told her he'd be teaching kids.

 "Jesus Christ," she simply said.

 "No shit," Andy agreed.

 And they shared a laugh.

Housing Provided

To promote camaraderie, foster cohesion, and reduce culture shock in general, many English schools house their foreign staff in the same neighborhood, often in the same tenement, and this English school is no exception.

Three floors tall, crammed between a pair of corporate high rises, our building stands like a fern among redwoods. There is no distinguishable entrance. A forsaken rear alley – forever shadowed, crumbled and dripping – leads to an unmarked door battered with dents and heavy scuffs. Nor is there an elevator. A fire escape. A lightbulb for the stairwell. An elderly "auntie" in a pink sun visor sweeps the apartments when a teacher moves out. Apart from that nothing is cleaned, fixed, replaced or maintained.

A coarse film of yellow pollution powders the stairs and handrails. Mice have eaten portals through the drywall. From the alley rises an assortment of tainted odors. Thin streams of oily discharge, imbued with tints of pink and green, trickle constantly into the sewer drains. Unless it is built for life in the shadows, no houseplant will survive here. The larger buildings keep all the sun for themselves. We are touched only by wind and rain.

Garbage is collected on Wednesday, though it has been three Wednesdays since last collection. A tumbling ridge of waste leans against the side of the building, its sacks gutted open by starving cats, pecked apart by grimy magpies.

The pigeons outside my window have no feet. Little deformed nubs like wads of chewed gum.

Parents

Sum-ni Jang would like to study at Princeton, but not as much as her mother would like it. Her mother wants it so badly she has enrolled her daughter in 8 extra hours of English instruction at Doctor Awesome. This in addition to the 15 weekly hours she gets at her private school. They have even named the family dog Princeton.

Sum-ni has dreamt of the Ivy League since she was a child. Her mother has dreamt of it since before Sum-ni was born. Her daughter's baby stroller was orange and black (Princeton colors) and her first toy was a plush tiger (Princeton mascot) dressed in a dapper black sweater printed with an orange "P." The tiger now dangles off the side of her backpack, fastened by a keychain, and I wonder which is the heavier load to haul: the weight of its symbolism or the books she carries?

At 17 Sum-ni is old enough to drive a car, but she will never be permitted to drive her social mobility. Her mother wears all the captain's hats on that vessel. She is Academic Manager, deciding when, where, and how much her daughter studies. She is Activity Coordinator, ensuring her daughter's involvement in all manner of extracurriculars which form the basis of a well-rounded admissions profile. She is publicist and spokesperson, circulating her daughter's achievements far and wide. And she is foremost Chief Architect, pouring into place all scholastic foundations that will lead her daughter to a postgraduate career in the Princeton University Economics Department.

But before Sum-ni can enter those almighty ivied walls she must first get into a top university in Korea. And before she can do that she must pass the National Entrance Exam. Not just pass it, her mother clarifies. Dominate it.

Sum-ni's mother is a senior advisor at Hankook Tire. The fifth largest tire company in the world, she explains. She tells me the ranking of the hospital in which her daughter was born and the private preschool from which she graduated. No less than twice a week does she track me down to probe Sum-ni's progress in composition and vocabulary. She has no interest in improvements. Her mission is to uncover deficiencies. Sum-ni waits to the side while we conference, deferring to mother's orchestration. Her life is lived without personal choice. Preparation, performance, obedience – that is the duty of her youth. And from what I can tell it is one she accepts benignly. Happiness is success, success is a pleased mother.

This evening Sum-ni's mother is not pleased. In the hall after class she grows aggressive in her pursuit of performance gaps. The National Exam is just four months away. The immense financial sacrifices – the premium schools, the academic camps, the costly glut of test prep courses – all of it will be justified or invalidated by her child's performance on that momentous day. Socially speaking, it is life or death. And faced with social death she offers me $80 an hour to provide her daughter one-to-one instruction. The girl has school from 8 to 5. After school there is clarinet training, badminton club, Doctor Awesome evening classes. But it is no trouble for Sum-ni to skip breakfast and be ready to learn at 7am.

The anxiety is appalling. I am appalled by these tiger mothers who enshrine their children but crave neither their friendship or appreciation, only their achievement. The woman leans forward as she solicits, so close I can see the gray roots of her hair. The force of her urgency tilts my shoulders back like a driving wind, and there is a moment where I almost cave, unable to withstand such vigor of fret. At the last instant I put her off, explaining that I am already overscheduled and recommending Andy as an alternative, something he may appreciate, for that extra $80 will help cover the rising cost of acid in Korea.

Sum-ni Jang would like to go to Princeton one day. And if by some miracle of grit and stamina she isn't eroded by the dismal cycle of events which constitute the educational experience here, then there's no reason to doubt she will do exactly that and more: for the rest of her life she will be able to overcome anything – anything whatsoever – that asks far too much of her.

Administration

When Director Choi was 23 her employer, a multinational electronics manufacturer, insisted she improve her English conversation skills, even though she worked in payroll and never interacted with English-speaking clients. She found a weekend language school for professionals, enrolled in an intermediate speaking class, and fell shockingly in love with the pale, grungy, Irish instructor with little blue gas lights for eyes.

The instructor was unfit to lead a classroom. He mumbled when he lectured, seemed unsure of his subject matter, and spent too much of his classes recounting his adventures backpacking in Thailand. But his eyes were blue fire. They absolutely blazed. And on those not infrequent mornings when the whites were bloodshot from a night's hard drinking, when the fume of alcohol leaked from his skin, the intensity of their blueness swelled like petrol thrown on a flame, and oh! – how impossible it became to fret about his credentials, his enunciation, the poor lessons in general.

He asked her out during an oral exam while impersonating a prospective employer. They sat across the table from each other in a cramped meeting room with fluorescent light buzzing overhead. His cologne was thick as dog breath and he wore his shirt with the top two buttons undone, the little coils of black chest fur intruding upon their dialogue.

She pretended to apply for an office job, something at a bank. He asked her to describe her greatest strengths, biggest weakness, and told her that his greatest weakness was pretty girls with long dark hair. Then he asked how she felt about romantic relationships between coworkers and whether she understood the terrible distraction she would cause by being so cute in the workplace. The blood tingled under her cheeks and she snickered with tension and encouraged the flirtation because it was all so rude and exhilarating, because no one with such eyes had ever looked intently upon her, because it was engrossing – overwhelming, in fact – to experience someone leveraging their authority to attract her. Boring little her. So she smiled and met him in his blue-flame eyes and said yes, she believed it was fine for coworkers to date.

There is more to tell, of course, though that is the most Director Choi has ever said about it. Nine years later her husband lives largely around Thailand, where he teaches English near beaches and sets his blue-flame sights on girls as silly for otherness as she used to be. Once a month he travels to Seoul to see his daughter and the three go shopping at malls or visit amusement parks. The child speaks no English, and as far as anyone knows, Director Choi plans to keep it that way.

Occasionally Director Choi will bring her daughter to work. The girl sits on the office floor and draws pictures of flying pigs in a sketch book. No one on faculty has heard her speak, and I, for one, have never seen her smile. Nor does she lift her gaze when I stop by to speak with her mother, who likewise does not smile and always, unfailingly, looks away from my blue eyes.

Pedagogy

For those who lack the training, the credentials, the years of critical study and experience, there is enthusiasm. Performed with theatrical volume, administered with backslapping vigor, an extreme dose of positive energy can neutralize any threat of intelligent questioning, suppress audacity, muzzle outspoken confusion, and conceal ineptitude or lack of preparation. So it goes with Intermediate Grammar.

Like a severed power cable Wayne State whips across the classroom, electric and crackling. You are all, he shouts, you are all kicking ass! He throws his fist as he spouts encouragement, beats it into his palm. On the whiteboard a sequence of exclamations, each one to be recited aloud. Yes you, Min-young. I am pointing to *you*. THE POLICE TOLD THE CROWD TO STAY BACK FROM THE HOUSE.

The students stare, faces blank. Almost everything remains inadequately grasped. Colloquialisms, especially. Prepositions of time and place. All those tiny parts of speech with complication and intricacy far out of proportion to their size. I would never – not for all the beer in Bavaria – take up the woe of English acquisition. The pronouns, the idioms, the conjugations and tenses. Though now and then we find a way to explain these competencies, we are for the most part as groping and uncertain as our students, possessed of native fluency, bereft of scholastic understanding. I would not dare – how can they do it? – fill my mouth with this second tongue. Yet they do. In swarms and throngs, they do. As the incoherent lessons amass, the weeks of incomprehension accumulate, one sees in their eyes, if bold enough to look, an equal piling of disgust and despair. Why can a man walk *slowly* but not *fastly*? Why does he have knees and toes but no *tooths* or *foots*? Why are clothes put on, never *put off*? And how can the same letters, spelled in the same order, form so many different pronunciations – as "cough" is *off* and "thought" is *ot* and "though" is *oh*. Until, my God, "enough" is *enuff*. Everyone, relax! For what you must understand is that most grammatical mistakes don't seriously affect communication.

    The students rise upon command, stand frozen at their desks as one by one they are called to recite the phrases on the board. It is a rare occasion when Wayne State is neither torpid with hangover nor anesthetized by pot, but in these moments he can put a pep squad to shame. Damn right! he roars. Almost all grammatical mistakes don't *seriously* affect communication. Why, you can screw up every preposition you ever use and a native speaker will still be able to understand you. What's important, children, is that you speak with confidence. Just say it!

    The message enlivens his mood with the force of a defibrillator, fills his being with buzzing conviction. He is a drum of gunpowder, their meekness his match spark. THE PIZZA HAS BURNED THE ROOF OF MY MOUTH. Again, Min-young. ENRICO HAS FALLEN ON THE BATHROOM FLOOR. Louder, Kang-joon. Enunciate, project!

    When each student has spoken aloud the board is erased, replenished with new sentences, and the drill repeated. Thus it goes with Intermediate Grammar. One more time. Everybody.

    You are all doing awesome!

Facilities

Here at Doctor Awesome we teach and learn in chicken stench. Pupil and master baptized in the Colonel's original recipe.

There is no escaping the deep steep. Morning to night our noses swim in the aroma of fried chicken parts. The classrooms reek of breaded thigh, of wing and breast and a side of hash. Up the stairs and through the air shafts the odors encroach. At peak dining hours their force constricts around us like a greasy bear hug. Apart from chicken we have stunk of scallion, egg, gizzards and garlic. What did I know of gravy's warm perfume? The effluvium of obesity's lair? I live my working life above Death's protein diet, and when I go home the stink of it goes with me, cooked into my hair and skin, baked into my clothes.

Director Choi remembers when the ground floor was a flower shop. There were roses in the window and pots of quilled chrysanthemums that reminded her of the blazing, disturbed stars of Van Gogh. Then one day the flowers were gone and the ubiquitous old white man in a dandy white suit, suspended in a frame of China red, was slapped against the side of the building. The new tenant was a stroke of fortune for Doctor Awesome. The adjacency of a KFC accentuated the school's international image. Hungry businessmen rushing to their evening classes could pop in and wolf down a carton of chicken tenders. Stranded students, waiting for their parents to pick them up, could idle in the dining area and play their handheld game consoles. Some parents enrolled their children based simply on the perk that the Colonel could serve as babysitter whenever they were running late.

Director Choi misses the flower shop but doesn't mind its replacement. When she was a girl a KFC appeared in her town like a child of prophecy and made everyone feel special and sophisticated. There'd even been a parade to welcome the franchise. Tickets were sold to the grand opening and somehow her father, a fixer of farm equipment, had gotten his hands on a pair. They'd queued for hours before crossing the threshold. Once inside her father swept her up in his arms and pointed at the mounted menu and said, "My daughter! We are taking a food tour of the United States. Isn't it fine!" And truly it was. They ordered a bucket of chicken – more than they could eat or afford – and dined in a booth by a window, neither of them enjoying the cuisine but delighting in their patronage, their first oily taste of western influence.

To this day Director Choi doesn't care for the food. But for the sake of nostalgia she will occasionally treat her daughter to a box of popcorn chicken or flaked-pastry tart topped with a scoop of whipped mashed. As for the smell, after so many years at Doctor Awesome she doesn't really notice it. Not that she would mind if she did. There are worse things in life than stinky chicken, she says. And certainly things that are greasier.

Housing Provided

The faculty residence contains fifteen efficiency hovels of identical dimension. The hovel across from mine contains Andy House.

Any comparison between Andy's apartment and a rat's nest would deeply demean most rats. Words fail it terrifically. The ten darkest poets could write 10,000 sonnets and never give life to its disarray.

Tonight's inventory is awing. Six uncapped milk cartons on the kitchen counter, spoiled dregs congealing. A dozen sauce-encrusted dishes crammed in the sink. Translucent strips of trampled noodles smeared across the floor. A toilet bowl rimmed with lime scale, stained with fecal streaks. A pair of yellowed underwear, visibly soiled, basking on the desk. A varied galore of unfinished junk food. Open bags of potato chips, half-eaten candy bars, paper tubs of instant ramen partly-filled with stagnant broth. On top of the television, a pizza box with petrified crusts and gnawed buffalo wing bones piled inside. As I stand around the room, sipping beer before we go out, I breathe mainly through my mouth, rarely the nose, for the air is ripe enough to make me woozy: a cloying, sour alchemy of body sweat, snack fart and tobacco smoke, the three interminably duking it out for top stench.

It is here, in this deranged sty, where Andy somehow seduces Korea. Here, with cultish fervor, that native girls perform a radical break from the rigorous tact of their conjugal homes, where they immerse in the weird pleasures of the West, plunge into its soiled and gluttonous waters, and where afterward they often send thank you gifts or tape love notes to the door.

What delight they find in Andy's lair, I have no idea. I only know that it must splinter them thrillingly from a life centered around orderliness and filial judgment. It is here in this apartment where a spurned young woman once abandoned all cultural modesty and came pleading in the middle of the night, crazed as an addict, beating her fist against the door, until at last Andy answered her cries, shirtless and high, pale belly sagging, and accepted her into his squalor.

Those who poked their heads into the hall to witness the scene had never seen anything like it. And it is nothing that anyone, not even Andy, knows how to explain.

English

A love of English literature will not, by itself, prepare one to teach the English language. It certainly will not prepare one to teach English in another country to those who don't already speak it. What good is a critical grasp of *Mrs. Dalloway*, what use a heightened acquaintance with Orwell, what practical service can any of it provide – all that hyper-intimacy with canonical hot shits – when tasked with explaining how English operates, at a chromosomal level, to rooms of children who have never expressed a complex sentence in their lives?

To the service of literacy there are many who devote their minds. You will not find them here. Dear children of a lesser pedagogue! Of dead authors and dusty prose I could evangelize, could spew like a whistling kettle. Surely I could move you to thirst, as I have learned to thirst, for stories that will enrich your perspective and clarify your connection with others. But to erect your proficiencies from scratch? To install the early infrastructure, the first paved pathways without which you can never venture beyond the elementary, to the wilds of Woolf and Atwood? That is no duty for this mere bibliophile.

I have been coldcocked by my inefficacy. Blindsided, knocked flat. Certainly there are those – older students especially – who have sensed to some degree that no educator of sophisticated merit would cross the earth to take employment at their inner-city cram school. Such cynicism they would never utter. It is in the eyes, soft seething like ember light, that I see it: the knowledge that they endure the winds of a native speaker, not a teacher. At least not one adept in the business of their great need.

I am not alone, of course, and I am far from anything new. A Buddhist from the Tang Dynasty once observed me so:

> A courteous young man,
> well-versed in classics and histories.
> People address him Sir,
> everyone calls him scholar.
> But he hasn't found a position
> and doesn't know how to farm.
> In winter he wears a tattered robe.
> This is how books fool us.

Students

Half past six, Friday night. All across the city the guests of a nation begin their public breathing.

In his left pocket Wayne State's cell phone steadily erupts: the chimed texts of restless chums plotting the evening's whoop-de-do. For the time has come to rummage for kicks, to swig hard and lurch forth, to make the mind a swamped, remorseless wad. Save your questions for Monday, Min-young. No more explanations tonight, Albert Lim. Shoo! Scat! Skedaddle! Be gone! This means you, Sun-mi. Forget the future tense. We have covered all that. You must take what we have covered and practice on your own. At home. Alone. Each of you. Away.

The students rise from their desks and file out of the room. By now they are used to it: the hasty dismissals, the impatience for clarifying questions. All resigned to their continuing incomprehension. All except Sun-mi Jang. In her eyes a mixed projection of determination and frost. She lingers alone in the room, combative in body language, ready to scratch and claw for clarity.

An erogenous dance song erupts in Wayne State's pocket. A custom ringtone reserved for an elusive hookup. The phone hums against his thigh, fills his crotch with dreaming. "I'm serious," he threatens. "Class dismissed, Sun-mi."

The girl anchors herself between Wayne State and the door, small fists ringing the hem of her shirt. She is barely a hundred pounds and sags under the weight of the books in her pack, but the force of her impatience is strong. She demands to know more about the simple future. Why is "I will reading" incorrect? What did teacher mean when he said "infinitive without to"?

Like a defensive end penetrating a line of scrimmage, Wayne State initiates a swim move, lobs his right arm over Sun-mi's head while nudging her aside with the left. She gives chase in the hall, her short legs keeping pace with his purposed strides. Down the stairs and through the door of the building, out onto the sidewalk; he cannot shake her. Why are some abbreviations pronounced as words and others letter by letter? What about prepositions of time and place? And why do we need the article "the" when talking about a specific thing when all the time people talk about *a* specific thing using the indefinite form?

For two blocks her questions pour forth in a roiling tumble. At last, trapped at the crosswalk, Wayne State turns and lifts a finger so close to her face that her eyes go crossed looking at it. "One more question," he says. "One more and I'll goddamn fail you."

The vile F-word produces its intended effect. Sun-mi's mouth clamps shut. She does not follow when he crosses the street. Later, at the bar, Wayne State laments.

"I hated to threaten her," he sighs. "But they have to learn, you know. For Christ's sake, somebody's gotta teach them."

Adult Conversation

Thursday evening is Adult Conversation. Six middle-aged executives still dressed in the suits they wore to work. All are here by mandate, compelled by their multinational employer to enroll in English enrichment courses. There is no expectation of improvement. A semblance of professional development is all that counts. Each arrives walloped by their workday. One with liquor on his breath and a slurred greeting. Nicely dressed though they are, nobody looks sharp. Their ties are loose and crooked, their collars greasy from the day's perspiration. Their hair sticks out in places, falls limp in others. One is so exhausted it seems as though his eyes will slide off his face.

Depending on one's commitment to learning goals, teaching businessmen can be anguish or reprieve, for the last thing they care about is learning. Tonight, like all nights, not a single person wants to be here. Inspired by the reek of their tipsy workmate, the class campaigns for a change of venue. What good is it to learn conversation in a classroom? Is that where people talk in real life? There is a place across the street where drinks are cheap and the Jazz is nice. And so we get drinks. Beer is brought to our table in a 2-liter tower with a plastic tap. Soon there is whisky. Between rounds the men hone their conversation skills. Sports: Am I fan of LeBron James? Food: Do I like kimchi? Sex: What do I think of Korean women?

The last topic dismantles the tedious routine of schoolbook English. There is a barrage of insinuating nudges and chuckles. One goes so far as to ask for a body count. Two? Three? Four? They are surprised, even disappointed, when I tell them none.

Sufficiently drunk, two of the men go home to their families. The rest of us find a public sauna to sweat the alcohol from our systems. The sauna, or *Jjimjilbang*, is gender segregated. Nude camaraderie, merry and rambunctious, everywhere the eye travels. As I undress at my locker a group of old men gather naked around me, saggy flesh steaming, drying their groins with scratchy white towels. One taps my shoulders with the back of his fingers, beckons me to face them. When I do they ponder my genitals with scrutinizing grunts, scholarly with interest, and suddenly I am the same self-conscious boy I was in middle school locker rooms, full of blush and awkwardness, worried about my lengths and symmetries, the fashion of my secret parts.

We soak together as a class. Though each of these men is a grown adult, it is nonetheless weird to bathe with students. I am quiet and tense in the bubbling tub, slightly woozy from the heat. After a while the drunkest of the class drifts to my side. He wraps a wet arm around my shoulder and asks if I would like to try a Korean woman tonight. It would be easy to find one. I refuse politely, citing fatigue, and he wags a finger in my face. "You are not tired, you are romantic," he teases. "Your love is somewhere else." But he is only partly correct.

Somewhere else, yes. Though nowhere I'm aware of.

Professional Development

Director Choi derives no pleasure from sufficiently upholding her position. Were it up to her she would intervene as little as possible in the underperformance of her western staff. But of course it is not up to her, and left to oversee our own professionalism we could not be counted upon to survive the scrutiny of the ferocious mothers whose obsession with the academic lives of their children is the basis for the school's existence. It is Director Choi's unenviable duty to face these women regularly and smooth their bristling criticisms, placate their concerns, and assure them of the value of a Doctor Awesome education when their children's English, and more pertinently their test scores, do not reflect it.

Thus, to bolster professional caliber – or at least the semblance of professional rigor – several quality control measures have been put into effect. From here on all faculty are subject to classroom observations and mandatory workshops to fortify practice. There is also a proficiency assessment. The assessment, proctored by Director Choi herself, is built of 30 multiple-choice questions which probe our mastery of syntax, grammar and diction. Bitterly, profanely – for the test is scheduled on a Saturday morning – all western staff attend and, for the most part, step and fetch. Only Wayne State, cognitively ransacked by his Friday night, openly snubs it. Bleary and reeking, he straggles into the room, selects C for every question, and finishes the exam almost as soon as he receives it.

On Monday Wayne State is summoned by Director Choi and informed of the situation. By answering C for every question he has scored a 13% and earned himself an immediate suspension. In the course of his reprimand it is revealed that the sole reason he hasn't been sacked and sent home with a revoked visa is because he is tall, blonde, and looks exactly the way management wants English to look. Of all the faculty he is the most physically prototypical, her David Beckham of subpar instruction.

But image only makes up for so much, and to avoid embarrassment he is given two books on English grammar and dismissed until he learns the rules of his own language. Enraged, Wayne State professes that he can ace any goddamn grammar test right there on the spot, but his scores and attitude are so poor that he has to suffer consequences. He will be excused without pay, required to take a make-up exam, and have his classes assigned to another teacher. And if he doesn't like it, Director Choi concludes, there are hundreds of international flights a day that will take him anywhere far, far away from her sight.

English

Two: a number denoting quantity. Too: an adverb indicating addition or extremity. To: a preposition expressing intention, condition, motion, you name it.

Their: the possessive form of *they*. They're: the combination of *they are*. There: as painfully slippery as *to*.

To keep things fun there is also by-buy-bye, heel-heal-he'll, where-wear-ware. Mug: a drinking cup, cylindrical in shape. Mug: to attack someone, usually to rob them. Well: to do something thoroughly, to be in good health, to behave in a proper manner, a way to start a sentence, a way to express surprise, a hole drilled into the earth to obtain oil or water, as well as gas (that is to say, in addition to). Make sense? Ah, well.

Wind is what blows against your neck or what a storm creates. Wind is what you do to a stopped clock when you want it to start. Sometimes the road winds. Sometimes we need to wind down. Sometimes we're out of wind.

Hungry? Why not have a pear for a snack? Or a pair of pears? Or a pair of pared pears?

Remember: "I before E except after C." Unless you're feeling *weird*. Or *seizing* the day. Or *being* yourself.

Our noses smell. So do our feet. Our feet run. So do our noses. Which reminds me: hamburgers are made of beef, not ham. Pineapples are neither apples nor found on pines. In the west, children, we drive on parkways and park in driveways.

And that's just the start of your English adventure!

Meet the Faculty

At midnight I am summoned to Andy's room. My colleague is in need. In a drunken trance he has misplaced three squares of acid and a ball of hash the size of a cocktail cherry.

The crisis has upheaved him. His mood like something flung up on the horns of a rampaging bull. Acid, in particular, is not easy to score in Korea and this stash has cost him half a month's salary. By the time I arrive he has ransacked his apartment, even pulling out the drawers in the kitchenette. The liquid of his eyes is crackling hot, like oil in a skillet. His face almost grotesque, as though a handsomer face has shrunken and withered. A single line of sweat crawls down his jaw, steady as a razor.

We lift his mattress, each of us hoisting one end at the same time. It is like removing the lid of a sarcophagus. Stale dust leaps up to meet us. Strange artifacts are exhumed: an old remote to a TV he no longer owns, a cell phone charger, a bottle of softgel hemp supplements that won't get you high. He snatches a jacket off the floor, flings it over his shoulder, scans the ground where it laid. He inspects the bathroom wildly, storms out and doubles back, inspecting it again. As the search goes on he begins to drag his hand heavily across his scalp and emit short, slurred profanities, seemingly involuntarily. With a shriek of fury he kicks a waste bin against the wall.

"Where is it?" he cries.

"The acid or hash?"

"All of it…Any of it. Goddamn it all!"

The outrage is menacing and in response I offer to search his bathroom again. I am scared to abandon him, afraid it will trigger a hostile response. And it is here I make a mistake. In an attempt to lighten the mood I joke that perhaps, in his drunken stupor, he decided to clean up his life and flush the whole stash down the toilet. The room falls quiet. He stands deathly still, watching me.

"Listen," he says. "You didn't touch my shit, did you?"

I laugh. He doesn't.

"Are you serious?"

"I understand if you did. You were just trying to help. But you have to tell me."

"You're out of your mind."

"You need to be honest."

The turn of his mind sends a chill spreading over my skin. I tell him I was joking, trying to be funny. I swear on my future grave that I do not care enough about him to help him clean up his life. But the seed of paranoia is planted and through his eyes I watch the slow recognition of an enemy envelop his brain like a shadow.

Now, if only to acquit myself, I am obliged to help him find his drugs. But there is no kill switch for what has been activated. His suspicion thickens like steam. He watches my movements. On his desk a tin box of shortbread cookies, a gift from one of his students. I pop the lid on the off-chance he stuck the drugs in there. When I turn around I am startled to find him standing behind me, a Phillips head screwdriver wrapped in his fist.

I pad my voice with gentle rationality, call his name. He does not seem to recognize my face. His eyes are glazed and barbaric, red like little war zones. When he takes a step toward me, it isn't in a *Let's chill and talk this out* kind of way. It's in a *If you don't give me my drugs I'm going to fucking stab you* kind of way. "Andy," I say again, and this time my breath goes short.

I slip my arm behind my back and grope the desk without being obvious. My hand finds something small and glass; I don't know what. But the item feels solid, heavy enough. I turn to the side like a pitcher in the stretch, concealing my loaded fist behind my hip. If he takes another step I will swing first to maximize my chances, will crack his animal skull.

The two of us look at one another, waiting. I hear every small sound of the apartment with terrible clarity. Andy shifts the screwdriver from left fist to right. Then, as if the motion has tripped his memory, the psychotic suspicion drains from his eyes and his mouth brightens like a Christmas light. The next instant he is in kitchen, shoving his face inside the toaster. With a victorious cry he flips the appliance upside down, shakes it over the counter. A baggie of acid and a ball of hash wrapped in foil tumble out. The acid he shoves in his pocket; the hash he unwraps and brings over for my appraisal, holding it out like a child who has captured a cricket. There is no apology, no humor or awareness of what just happened. A happy peace encloses him.

The object in my fist is a glass ashtray. I am still clutching it tightly when he lights the hash and fills his lungs, tender smoke floating out of his face.

Students

In-young and Min-soo are BFFs. They don't need anyone else. They sit at the back of Intermediate Speaking and laugh behind their hands at what other students say. Most days they sleep facedown on their desks or nuzzle together to gossip over celebrities on their phones. Their English is the worst in the class, and on the rare occasion when called upon to answer a question they lock eyes with one another and screw their faces into squinting smirks, as if asking them to contribute is the silliest thing teacher could do.

At a time when all their peers are writhing under the pressure of national exams and mutating into parental expectations, In-young and Min-soo defy configuration. School life and its evaluative norms mean nothing. They have no drive to be first, do not care about assessment, and are by far the happiest students I have taught at Doctor Awesome.

Once on the way to class I caught them playing a game at the bottom of the stairs – something like Rock, Paper, Scissors. At the count of three each girl threw their hand into a shape of their choosing. When one girl lost, the other ascended a certain number of steps while the loser remained where she was. They giggled like lunatics, shaking their fists into shapes again and again, until at last In-young had won so many times that the entire staircase stretched between them.

The two stood at opposite ends calling out to one another, In-young at the top, Min-soo at the bottom. Then a troubling notion seemed to stab In-young and her face grew anguished. She called Min-soo's name, almost desperately, and at the sound of her voice all levity left Min-soo's expression and both girls became still and quiet where they stood.

Then it was like In-young had not seen her friend in years, and she flew down the stairs in a greedy rush and grabbed Min-soo's arm. A flood of laughter burst from their lungs and they spoke Korean to one another and laughed some more. Then they linked arms at the elbows and walked out of the building. Just turned and left school without any explanation, without a look in my direction, and did not come back. Not that day or any day since. I have no idea what has happened to them, and damned if I've ever marked them absent.

Housing Provided

The Canadian on the third floor sells mescaline and hash. The Irishman down the hall can get you methocarbamol. There is an Aussie, a psychotropic purist, who peddles envelopes of fragmented fungus. Shriveled red mushroom caps and occasionally salvia.

On Sundays Wayne State buys enough weed from a West African to make it through the week. Sometimes when Andy drops acid he descends into a ghost town deep inside his toilet drain. A place of absolute loneliness. Sometimes he screams from a vat of boiling dyes.

Sometimes you can buy painkillers from the Californian up the hall whose Korean girlfriend won't sleep with him. More educated than most, he has translated Neruda love poems into Hangul and plans to recite them over wine. If that doesn't work, the Irishman can get him rohypnol.

Meet the Faculty

    Too much grievance goes unexpressed, pinned beneath this fear of sanctimony. How can a pilgrim feel proud of what he is, where he's from, when so thickly surrounded by the most dysfunctional of his kind?

    At closing time tonight Wayne State stops to urinate on a rack of bicycles. He stands bent at the knees, holding his genitals with one hand, the other braced against the concrete well of a city-planted tree. His belt is undone, zipper flaps fully splayed. As he relieves himself he sways in gentle circles and rocks on his heels, the stream of his urine swerving from side to side.

    The people walk by in their nightlife clothes, pretending not to see. Pretty couples holding hands or sharing cups of gelato. When he has emptied his bladder he removes his shirt and propositions a caucus of girls waiting for a taxi. He is largely incoherent; only the most vulgar words are discernable. When the cab pulls up he makes a move to get inside, belt and fly still undone. But he is too slow and blundering, too clobbered by double bourbons, and when the girls shut the door he smashes his fist against the roof and throws a punch at the car.

    He staggers alongside as the vehicle accelerates, cursing through the window, then trips over his feet and drops like a grain sack. Too disoriented to pick himself up, he flounders in the road, flopping fish-like in traffic. More than once he is nearly struck by a scooter.

    From piss to face-plant the folly takes less than two minutes. But in that time the full provenance of my flight to Korea plays out in my mind. It was Southside Boston, a place diseased to its deepest marrow with sports and religion, where I started dreaming of the road, my apartment so damp and ill-heated that I wore my thickest coat the entire winter, even to bed. A vicious nor'easter getting through the window one evening and soaking all my books. How spitefully I had arranged them on the ledge so that neighbors would see that not everyone on that street was diseased like them – they who decorated their windows with Tom Brady jerseys and Red Sox pennants. A rancorous, data-logging, entry-level English grad crying, at 27 years old, at the sight of thousands of sopping pages, the wise inks hopelessly bled. Books that had duped and suckered me and ripped my life away, but they were things I'd finished and I loved them for that.

And there was a day, an unblemished September afternoon, when I fled the city on a whim and drove to the Cape because I'd heard it was a place where people flourished. I wanted to see the nice homes by the water that were only occupied a few congenial months a year, the prosperous New England families digging for clams, kicking back in custom Adirondacks with their swishing dune grass vistas.

And I knew when I got there I would resent whatever I saw, but went anyway because I thought it would be good for me, confronting what I hadn't reached – thought it would be good because I was tired of the corrosive strain of envy. I would look success in its sandy, sunny-blue face and resign myself to my absence of prospects, my abundance of unavailing competency, and I would move on.

That is what I thought, though it makes no sense to me now.

And when I got there I found a private road with an ocean at the end of it, and I drove down the road and parked behind a wreck of bleached driftwood. And beyond the driftwood were heaps of dune grass like puppies under a blanket, ropes of seaweed torn up by the roots. And through a swale in the mounds I could see the cool Atlantic and smell its odor, hear its salt breeze lick against my car. And I waited. Waited for something marvelous to induce my reconciliation. And eventually it appeared: a pleasure boat tooling through the shallows, captained by a golden Hercules in a denim cowboy hat. By his side stood three sirens in two-piece bikinis, each with full gleaming breasts and sun shining through their hair. They skimmed across the ocean with green-bottle beers in their hands, their beautiful mouths pouring golden noise into the world. Every few seconds one of them would run a finger inside the crack of her rump and snap the thong back into place.

And I saw, too, a handsome family eating sushi on a picnic bench: a mother and father and two blonde daughters. I watched from my car, following the flow of chatter pass between their mouths of rice and raw sea meat. Watched with a kind of anthropologic enchantment, as though studying the ways of a secret people. And there was soda in glass bottles and bowls of dipping sauce, and a white tablecloth held down by four beach stones at every corner. And napkins. Big, bright lavender napkins pinned beneath father's wallet to keep the wind from blowing them away.

And when the sushi was gone and it was time to wipe lips and chins, father lifted his wallet and the napkins leapt on the back of a sudden gust and fled across the shore. Up-up-and-away the wild napkins flew, whirling like drunken bonfire sparks. They rose in writhing arcs, crashed down in the wild rye, rose again. And the girls squealed and bolted like hounds in pursuit. Laughing, shrieking, ruthless with amusement, they stamped the napkins under their feet and snatched them out of the air, holding their quarry high for mother and father, who called out with white lightning smiles and raised their glass sodas as the girls collapsed into the grasses and sprang to life again and again, breathless and waving.

And in the presence of this spectacle my spite and sanctimony did not diminish, but enlarged as though injected with a powerful steroid. And how crabbed and ugly the future seemed just then; how homely and sputtering my reality when set beside these lives; and how vigorously I put that indignation to my brain and blew myself to Korea and a new diaspora of floundering shitshow.

With the help of strangers Wayne State rises to his feet. He teeters like a boat at anchor, muttering at honking traffic, stunned by the light and movement of the world. The thought of his companionship is suddenly unbearable, and I turn and walk anywhere from his direction. I do not look back. I walk without destination into a part of the city I have never been, turning left on random streets, veering right at others. There is nothing ahead I wish to reach, only something behind that projects me forward. And with each step my aimless escape grows more foreboding. Not because it is so strange, but because it is so familiar.

Administration

Before they were married, Director Choi's husband would tell stories about Ireland and pledge to bring her back and make her a citizen one day. On occasion she recalls the Korean BBQ they were going to open in Galway.

Now at 37 it is difficult to imagine a time when her outlook might have possessed even a granule of such optimism. Almost daily she bears enough stress to weigh down a mule. Inadequate pay, overwhelming hours, and a punishing commute have warped her default expression into a bleary glower. Rigorous servility in the line of duty has likewise taken its toll. In addition to placating obsessive parents she must appease a wholly male senior management, assume blame when not at fault, meet expectations without resources, and put together a pleasurable and positive learning environment with a largely uninspired and uncommitted faculty. Most of her work weeks contain 80 hours and none contain less than 60. She works when she is sick. She works on painkillers for migraines. She works first thing in the morning after working late the night before. By mid-afternoon the force of her exhaustion projects into every exchange. Its density is astounding. And there is simply no question that at certain points during the day she is deeply unexcited about remaining conscious.

Yet from the ashes of this burnout a beautiful spectacle is sometimes born. For every so often Director Choi crumbles like a sinkhole to the steep misbalance of her life; and in these moments there is neither sobbing nor tirade, but rather a ferocious gluttony for jubilation. Suddenly the continental rift is closed and we are summoned to celebrate – Korean staff and western faculty – brought together over thin slices of barbequed meat and emerald bottles of soju, over cheap whiskey and plaintive love songs in a strobe-lit karaoke den. At intervals throughout our intemperance a pitiful use of chopsticks, cheeky cultural faux-pas, or butchered song note will delight Director Choi to hysterics. The head tips back; the face crinkles in joy. Her wits erupt like pyroclastic surge. It is a tear-squinting, stomach-clenching, asphyxiating phenomenon from which there is no easy recovery. When Director Choi comes back from elation she is daffy, blinded, and struggles for air. She cannot speak clearly for several moments and grows just a bit drowsy. Then it is like a soft wind sifting through feathers. The bleary glower of her face, all her features, are lifted and rearranged.

    It is remarkable mirth, truly. I have never seen dejection so scoured. And for the rest of the evening there is, at least for me, no prettier attraction than the sight of her mind spoiled for somber thought, dazed in rejoice, which one can tell by the weightless, far-away light that lingers on her face.

Special Topics in English Conversation
By Andy House

Have you ever wondered about that lump of crud that comes out of your body when you sit on the toilet? That's shit. Shit is everywhere in the world: in our bodies; on the sidewalk. Maybe you've even stepped in it! But did you know that shit is part of our conversations? Shit comes out of our mouths everyday. It's in our governments and schools! Many religions and laws are made entirely out of shit. And you know what else? Nothing in the world has more shit than English! Here's a taste of just how much shit there is to learn!

1) <u>Bullshit</u> = a mass of lies and deception.
   - This job contract is bullshit! We never get paid when we're supposed to!
2) <u>Chicken Shit</u> = a cowardly person.
   - Don't be a chicken shit! Tell your parents you hate English.
3) <u>Give a Shit</u> = to not care about something.
   - If you think I give a shit about this job, you're crazy.
4) <u>Good Shit</u> = good drugs, good marijuana, good pills.

- I'm looking for some good shit in Korea.
- I'm not joking. Send me a text if you know where I can get good shit around here.

5) <u>Holy Shit</u> = something you say when you're surprised.
- Holy shit! You're pregnant?!

6) <u>Deep Shit</u> = serious trouble.
- I got the girl pregnant and now I'm in deep shit.

7) <u>Beat the shit</u> = hurt someone physically and badly.
- The girl's father wants to beat the shit out of me.

8) <u>Little shit</u> = a weak, incapable, insignificant person.
- How's a little shit like him going to fight me?

9) <u>Scare the shit</u> = to be badly frightened.
- Most people around here don't know what they're doing with their lives and it scares the shit out of them.

10) <u>Shit-faced</u> = very drunk.
- I drank six beers and five shots of tequila. I was shit-faced when I told her I loved her.

Topics for Discussion

1) Tell us about a time when you heard bullshit from someone at school/in this class/at home.

2) Who do you know who is a chicken shit?

3) Who do you give a shit about? Who don't you give a shit about?

4) Do you know a little shit at work or school?

5) Have you ever beat the shit out of someone?

6) Are you going to get shit-faced tonight?

7) Is Andy shit-faced now?

8) Where can you get good shit in Korea? Does Andy know?

Parents

Today is the day that Sum-ni's mother goes out of her way to believe in God. Tomorrow her daughter sits the National Entrance exam. Tomorrow her child's worth and future, to say nothing of the family's merit, will be determined for all to see. Every class, quiz, test and assignment – every hour of every lesson Sum-ni has gruelingly sat through – has been preparation for this. There is nothing more a mother can do. All power to tip the balance of fortune in her child's favor is disabled. The impotence is terrifying.

Bereft of an earthy outlet for involvement she shifts her focus to the Big Proctor in the sky. For three hours this afternoon she occupies the front pew of her Catholic church, entreating a mounted crucifix, reminding the Almighty of her charitable contributions, her consistent attendance at church, her purity as wife and mother. Of God she asks nothing unreasonable. Only that her daughter make her proud. Tomorrow she will get the day off work to stand outside the exam center as the test-takers file into the building to fulfill or fail outrageous expectations. Hordes of parents and kinfolk shouting encouragement, singing heroic songs, raising homemade banners. Their children will march by like soldiers parading before deployment. While not all will return victorious, surely Sum-ni will. As sure as God is honorable, her mother ordains. All she has done for the sake of faith was purposed toward success on this day. It is time for heaven to pay up.

Tonight, the night before the exam, Sum-ni asks if I might stay a moment after class and review the future tense. We sit alone at the desk while I write examples in her notebook. All my stores of patience are brought to surface. I am full of tenderness for this girl, who with every passing moment seems as though she will buckle to the pressure within her, her bones crumbling in on themselves like a slab of glacier collapsing into the sea. How the weight of their filial piety does not break these children, I will never understand.

When our time is up she does not want to leave. Beyond this room looms a thing she is unready to face. She slips her notebook into her pack and the two of us sit awkwardly, looking at one another. No need to say good luck, I tell her. I know she will do just fine. As the words leave my mouth I am stricken by the sheer inadequacy of my wisdom. Are such boilerplate encouragements all I have to offer in the face of someone's needful angst? The girl, too, is deflated by the attempt. Rising heavily, she offers a perfunctory bow, says, "Thank you, teacher," and vanishes toward her fate. In her wake the room is silent, empty. Only me at the desk, lingering in the reek of chicken.

Though like Director Choi I am beginning not to notice it.

Contract Completion

Faculty drama at the Doctor Awesome English Academy. Wayne State is nowhere to be found. For three days his phone goes unanswered. So does his door. He has missed a meeting with Director Choi and the make-up assessment that would end his suspension. Some fear he is injured in his apartment, perhaps unconscious. Those who know him best suggest he has puked in his sleep and choked.

A call is made to the building manager. Director Choi waits in the hall while maintenance opens the apartment with a master key. The place is trashed and cluttered with trite possessions – cups, dishes, linens, stolen office supplies. But the standing wardrobe is bare, the clothes and suitcases gone. In the waste bin by the desk, two grammar workbooks.

The investigation wraps up quickly. It is determined by Director Choi that in the style of disgruntled *waeguks* Wayne State has jumped his contract, emptied his bank account, and hopped a plane to God knows where. It happens two or three times a year, says Director Choi, and she knows the signs.

At a rock bar in Hongdae, Led Zeppelin wailing from the speakers, we raise our booze to our former colleague and recount his legacy. All the times he taught high, boggered on pills or dope; all the times he taught drunk, still wrecked from the night before; that one morning after passing out on a public basketball court when, so hazed and sick and numb to consequence, he arrived to class in the pants he'd pissed while unconscious.

It is because of Wayne State, we note, that our classes are now monitored and why our lesson plans must be pre-approved by Director Choi. Wayne State, instructor and comrade, whose eternal proximity to his adolescence inspired lectures on euphemisms like "bumping uglies" and "jamming the clam.." And who, for no perceivable reason but spiteful mischief, once taught a class of middle-schoolers that it was only appropriate to use intransitive verbs when they were physically *in transit*, never at rest. An amusing abuse of trust if we forget that there are now dozens of learners primed for ignorance and embarrassment down the road. Or, pitiably, even if we don't forget.

Happy Hour

Many places in Asia make Las Vegas seem like an Amish hamlet, and this place is occasionally one of them.

Subway line six carries us to Itaewon-dong, Western Town. At some point the US installed a military base here. Then the armed forces got bored and the usual enterprises piled into the area to make bank off that boredom. Dance clubs arrived. So did bars and liquor stores. Then prostitutes, salon girls, hourly motels and movie rooms with straw beds. Now every building is layered to the roof with taverns and massage parlors. Now, on any given night, one can behold a nebula of ex-pats drifting through the mystifying space of Korea, of Asia in general, each of us looking to be solaced or stimulated, ecstasized or destroyed. The night pulses with solicitation; the flash-blink of neon signage, the throb-beat of club music. Bar girls in heavy makeup pass out flyers for shows while foreign hustlers, hovering in blackened doorways, pitch their services with guarded murmur.

At a penthouse hookah lounge we rendezvous with Andy's friends: two teachers from Scotland looking for group sex. By midnight the table is a jumbled airstrip of beer mugs and cocktail glasses. Dark pints of European stout take off from the bar and land before our faces. A bottle of Johnnie Walker taxis between our lips. Group sex isn't easy in Korea, Andy explains. They will have to try hookers, no salon girls. Andy is addressing the matter exuberantly, snapping his fingers at different ideas, delighting in the challenge of a tricky flesh adventure.

But it is not to be. Near closing time the Scots clip shoulders with an American soldier. A punch is thrown, glass breaks on the floor; several bodies, bouncers and bar folk lump into a scrum. Andy does not engage. A steady fire of flirty emojis hammers his phone. Forsaking the Scots, we slip out the entrance and make our way to a plaza fountain, where a young girl in a strapless romper waits by the spattering water, dark eyes bright with bashful tension. She has roughly 50 words of English in her possession and giggles at the cootchie-coo that drizzles over her from Andy's mouth. At moments it seems as though it is all too much for her, that she would like to turn and flee but cannot detach herself from the strangers she has opened her life to. And in this way we are linked, this girl and I. Each of us uneasily enthralled, like gawkers at a circus, by this swinging plowbilly daredevil who has come trapezing into our lives.

We fill our guts with barbequed food: slices of sautéed garlic and cucumber, dripping strips of marinated pork. The girl's eyes are like a newborn fawn's, alert and overwhelmed by the environment. In time her face turns scarlet from beer. Hesitation dissolves into a kind of tantalized absorption. Andy's fingers strum her bare thighs. Leaning close, he speaks of ecstasy, asks if she has ever known the joy of being loved by the world or kissed another person and felt the tingle of their galaxies, their billions of inner stars pass through her tongue and fill her universe with fizzy pleasure. She watches his mouth as he talks, trying to piece together meaning. The only words seemingly comprehended are *love* and *kiss*.

From here the night veers from the conventional derelictions of the main drag to the twisting ancestral alleys, where the dark indulgences are sold. No longer capable of sober companionship but unsure of how to exit the night, I tag along as Andy infiltrates one hangout after another, searching for a dealer. As I tag along I begin to understand that seduction is largely a matter of breaking a person of their training. It is seizing a clean, obedient soul by the hand and introducing it to sketchy misadventure at three in the morning, to broken alleys and leering cons and the succulent dopamine of free-swimming behavior. There is no chatting over coffee or strolling at the zoo. No gradual fall. Only a straight plummet into the imperfectly known and a swift, not wholly certain yank of the ripcord at the last minute.

    At 4am Andy sniffs out a buzz-cut Texan with a cache of psychoactives the color of sweet tarts. The Texan is part of that idle military presence that must forever be ready to drill and simulate when the cretin across the DMZ fires a missile at the ocean. Away from base he looks like a kid in detention: flat-billed ballcap twisted sideways, boxers hoisted above baggy jeans. The transaction is handled in the secrecy of a public restroom. When Andy returns he places a single pink tablet in the girl's palm, asks if she is ready to enter a world of love. I am not invited.

    They place their tablets on their tongues and swallow. When the pill has slid down her esophagus the girl reaches for Andy's wrist, not wanting to be left alone with whatever will happen next. I do not follow when they vanish down the stairs of an underground disco, grabbing at each other's skin.

    Later at home I vomit into the toilet. On my hands and knees, face in the bowl, I breathe the mess of my digestion. What was once inside me is sour and sludge-like. I am startled by the strong, foul smell of it.

English

Almost daily the students are reminded of its global apotheosis. English: the language of diplomacy; English: the language of trade. In such vague, enormous assertions they are told it is the de facto speech of opportunity. But nobody likes a colonized mouth. Their tongues have been invaded, overrun by a Roman alphabet. It is English school in the morning. English school at night. English on weekends and during vacation. Along with English, students are taught western geography, western civics, western history and politesse. The harder questions go unanswered. "Why are English books translated into Korean but Korean books not translated into English?" "Why do westerners not learn Hangul? You are the ones coming *here*."

Little do they know how dearly their parents pay to have them stripped of their natural speech. The home language is neither celebrated nor encouraged. Rarely is it acknowledged. Like understaffed factories their tiny mouths struggle to produce the quota of syllables required for each sentence. Their tongues fatigue, their voices drag. Ordained to view themselves through a lens of deficit, it is no wonder how thoroughly they lose interest in their lessons. And I am out of touch – that is no small part of it. As digital natives, their brains are wired differently. And though it would help to embrace their media and technologies, I am too overwhelmed by what they know to recalibrate my approach, to ditch my dated methodologies. Repetition, rehearsal, drill. That is the way we learn.

By hour's end even the threat of low marks fails to motivate. There is nothing to do but cut them loose. The steel press of education lifted from their souls, they burst from their seats and gallop down the stairs, cracking the air with high screeching voices. The unbridled rapture emphasizes their loathing for the subject matter. It is by no means rare to see six or seven of them nearly crushed by traffic as they bolt deer-like into the city and make their escape from English.

Students

How best to describe Elena Kwon? A girl who has been nowhere and retained everything. The ancient wonders and modern marvels, the Vatican and the Louvre, the Great Barrier Reef. Only the best of every destination has been enshrined in her dream hall – of Paris especially. Cultured strolls through covered arcades, brasserie fare along the Champs Elysees, lovers embracing in Baroque gardens.

On her phone after class Elena shares images of Santorini, steeped in Aegean blue, towns of whitewashed homes flowing over coastal slopes. One day when her English is strong she will visit places like Paris and Greece and take the world into her soul. Strange, I know. But she believes it. As if English is a galloping rider that will sweep her onto its horse and carry her to her horizons of desire.

It is in this spirit that she misidentifies me. Projecting the romantic generalities of her bohemian dreams, she finds me a fascinating figure, a Gulliver that has entered her land of Lilliputians. My westerness equates to prolific exposure to everywhere and everything, to a mind enamored with the diversity of existence; and, at least today, it is more than I can stand. No, I have never travelled to Greece. No, I have never ascended Machu Picchu. No, Elena Kwon, I have never hiked the El Camino or toured the stately rubble of Roman civilization.

Such paucity of exploration is hard to believe. How could anyone decide to live and work in another country, to undertake such a stupefying cultural transition, without an itch for expedition or compulsion to roam? I do not know how to explain that it is possible – indeed, entirely universal

– to end up among extraordinary otherness without ever having an interest in being there. Not that my explanation would mean anything. Not to Elena Kwon. When this one reaches the otherness of her dreams it will be on the fuel of prodigious curiosity, not a sickness toward home.

    The next day her fancy falls on New York City. What can I tell her of Broadway and Central Park? Of countdowns and confetti in Times Square? Have I ever watched the ball drop, warmly bundled in winter fashion, and kissed my love at the first stroke of a new beginning?

About Us

My time with Andy runs short. Now Mongolia is calling. There is a teaching job in Ulaanbaatar; a Kazakhstani girl whose been sending nude pics for a month.

We are somber this final night together, as though feeling ourselves grappling with a complexity about which the other knows nothing. It is a back alley hookah bar. There is a bottle of rice wine and two stone bowls from which to drink. We sit outside on plastic stools, smoking floral tobacco from a shared hose. A plump white moth circles the street lamp overhead, beating its brains against the light. Andy's drags are slow and gentle, as are his exhalations. Fragrant smoke rises from his lips in lethargic streams. On top of the pipe, burning red in a clay bowl, a charcoal puck heats the jasmine shisha. Now and then the waitress attends our table and turns the puck with a pair of tongs, baffled and skeptical, as though she cannot fathom what we are doing in this back-alley dump with so many astonishing places to be. Andy watches the moth and begins.

"When I was growing up in Missouri we had these snapper turtles. They were always getting into our ponds and nobody liked them, so we killed them whenever we could. This one day a snapper crawled into our yard and my mom said I could have a go at it. So I took an axe and started hacking its shell. But I was little. I couldn't lift the blade over my head. So I held it by the throat and just hacked with little blows till I cracked its shell. It was still alive but I was tired and didn't care anymore, so my mom said to get rid of it and I chucked it into the road. Well, this truck came by and pulled over and this fella in overalls got out and picked up the snapper and said, 'Hey, boy. You want this snapper?' I told him no. So he threw it in the back of his truck and when I asked what he was going to do with it he said, 'Cook it,' just like that, and drove away. It was just this dirty hacked-up turtle lying in the road but he was my people and was going to eat it. So as soon as I was old enough I got the hell out of there. Just took off and kept going and going. Except, wherever I ended up, it was never far enough away from that. You know? I mean, goddamn. You get what I'm trying to say?"

    I do not know how to answer. And before I can say anything he swipes at the air and returns his gaze to the moth. Our English isn't suited for such discussion, and we cast the language aside and devote ourselves with greater diligence to our silence and heavy smoking. Our bowls of sour wine.

About the Author

Timothy Laurence Marsh is a writer, educator and wayfarer who splits his time between the U.S. and Latin America, where he teaches film and writing at Texas Tech University–Costa Rica. His work explores the bizarre intersections of place and the pursuit of meaning in chaotic systems, whether in classrooms, foreign countries, or the human heart. His stories have appeared in Catapult, The Rumpus, Fourth River, The Los Angeles Review, Cream City Review, and Coolest American Stories 2025. Connect with him at timothylaurencemarsh.com or on Twitter/X: @TLMarsh7.

www.ingramcontent.com/pod-product-compliance
Lightning Source LLC
LaVergne TN
LVHW050029080526
838202LV00070B/6977